THIS WALKER BOOK BELONGS TO:

_____

_____

_____

_____

For Rosaleen
M.W.

For Dad
J.B.

First published 1991 by
Walker Books Ltd, 87 Vauxhall Walk
London SE11 5HJ

This edition published 1993

2 4 6 8 10 9 7 5 3

Text © 1991 Martin Waddell
Illustrations © 1991 Jill Barton

Printed in England

British Library Cataloguing in Publication Data
A catalogue record for this book is
available from the British Library.

ISBN 0-7445-3049-0

THE HAPPY HEDGEHOG BAND

Written by

Martin Waddell

Illustrated by

Jill Barton

WALKER BOOKS
LONDON

Deep in the heart
of Dickon Wood lived
a happy hedgehog
named Harry.

Harry loved noise
so he made a big drum
and he banged on the drum
tum-tum-te-tum.

A hedgehog called Helen
was out in the wood.
She heard
tum-tum-te-tum
and she liked it.

So she made a drum
and went off
to join in the drumming.

And so did a hedgehog
named Norbert
and another called Billy;
they both made drums

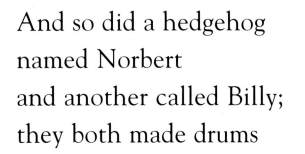

and followed the
tum-tum-te-tums,
until all of the hedgehogs
with drums
were gathered together
at Harry's.

Tum-tum-te-tum
went one drum;
that was Harry.

Diddle-diddle-dum
went one drum;
that was Helen.

Ratta-tat-tat
went one drum;
that was Norbert.

And
BOOM
went one drum;
that was Billy.

Tum-tum-te-tum
diddle-diddle-dum
ratta-tat-tat
BOOM
Tum-tum-te-tum
diddle-diddle-dum
ratta-tat-tat
BOOM

The whole wood
was
humming
and
tumming
with drumming.

"STOP!"

cried the pheasant,
the owl and the bee,
the mole from his hole
and
a badger called Sam
and his mother,
and the fox and the crow,
the deer and the dove,
the frog and the toad
and the spider
and
the dog
who was lost
in the wood.

Tum
went the band
and they STOPPED!

"We want to play too!"
said the others.
"But we haven't
got drums.
So what can we do?"
And nobody knew
except Harry.

Harry knew all
about noise.
So he said,

you can buzz,

you can hoot,

"You can hum,

you can pop.

you can click,

you can clap,

you can whistle,

We'll carry on with the drums."

And ...

they did.

And the dog
who was lost
in the woods
just danced.

Tum-tum-te-tum
diddle-diddle-dum
ratta-tat-tat

BOOM